Beverly Cleary

TWO DOG BISCUITS

Illustrated by
DyAnne DiSalvo-Ryan

A Young Yearling Special

Published by
Dell Publishing Co., Inc.
1 Dag Hammarskjold Plaza
New York, New York 10017

ISBN: 0-440-49134-7

Reprinted by arrangement with William Morrow and Company, Inc.

Printed in the United States of America

November 1987

10 9 8 7 6 5 4 3 2

D

Now that Jimmy and Janet are four years old they can do lots of things. They can draw pictures of funny bugs and birthday cakes and eggs in a nest.

They can sing *Skip to My Lou*. They can pump themselves up high in their swings, and they can swat flies.

Jimmy and Janet are twins. This means they have the same father, the same mother, and the same birthday, too.

They get up at the same time and go to bed at the same time.

Janet always has Jimmy to swing with her on the glider, and Jimmy always has Janet to sit on the other end of the teeter-totter.

"I think twins are a very nice arrangement," said Mother. "What does 'very nice arrangement' mean?" asked Janet, who liked big words.

"It means I am glad I have twins," answered Mother. Jimmy and Janet think twins are a nice arrangement, too.

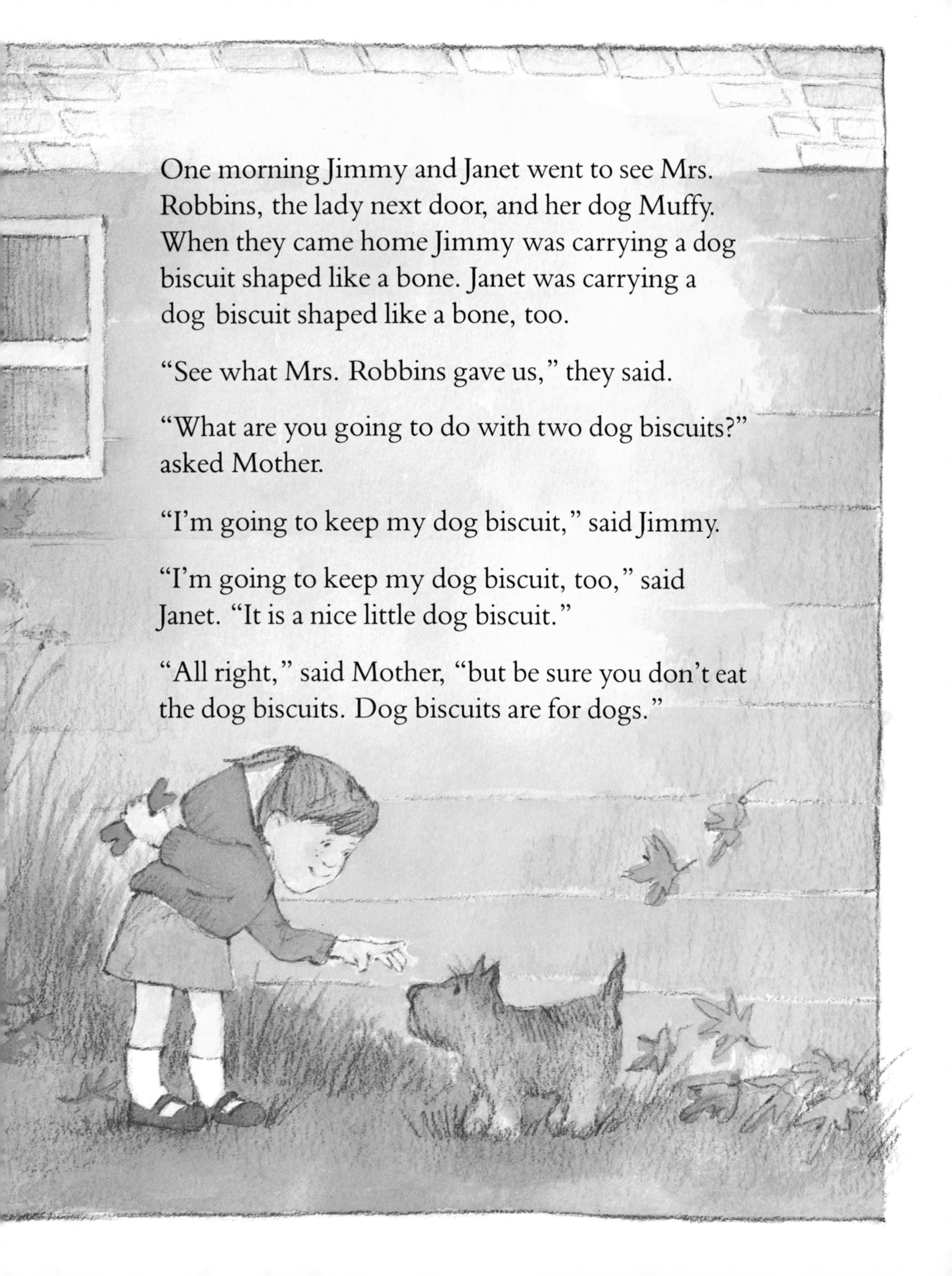

One morning Jimmy and Janet went to see Mrs. Robbins, the lady next door, and her dog Muffy. When they came home Jimmy was carrying a dog biscuit shaped like a bone. Janet was carrying a dog biscuit shaped like a bone, too.

"See what Mrs. Robbins gave us," they said.

"What are you going to do with two dog biscuits?" asked Mother.

"I'm going to keep my dog biscuit," said Jimmy.

"I'm going to keep my dog biscuit, too," said Janet. "It is a nice little dog biscuit."

"All right," said Mother, "but be sure you don't eat the dog biscuits. Dog biscuits are for dogs."

Janet laid her dog biscuit on a chair. Jimmy laid his dog biscuit on the couch. When Mother started to sit on the couch, she asked, "Whose dog biscuit is this?"

“My dog biscuit,” answered Jimmy, and put his dog biscuit on the kitchen table. Janet put her dog biscuit on the kitchen table, too. She did not want Mother to sit on her dog biscuit.

At lunchtime Mother said, “Put your dog biscuits away, children. I don’t want you to get mixed up and eat them for lunch. Dog biscuits are for dogs.”

Jimmy and Janet put their dog biscuits in their pockets.

After lunch and naps Mother said, "It's time for some clean clothes." When Jimmy took off his jeans, his dog biscuit fell out of his pocket. When Janet took off her coveralls, her dog biscuit fell out of her pocket, too.

"My goodness," said Mother. "Every place I look I see dog biscuits. Why don't you take the dog biscuits next door and give them to Muffy?"

"Muffy has dog biscuits," said Janet. "He has a big bag of them."

"Then give the dog biscuits to some other dog," said Mother.

"Dogs don't come to our house," said Jimmy.

"Then let's go find a dog," said Mother. "Put on your clean clothes, and we'll go for a walk and find a dog that would like two dog biscuits."

So Jimmy and Janet, wearing their clean clothes, went for a walk with Mother. "Be on the lookout for a dog," said Mother.

"What does 'be on the lookout' mean?" asked Janet.

"It means to watch for something," answered Mother. Jimmy and Janet and Mother were on the lookout for a dog.

The first dog they met was a big brown dog. "I don't want to give my dog biscuit to a brown dog," said Jimmy.

"I don't want to give my dog biscuit to a big dog," said Janet.

"Oh, dear," said Mother. "I guess we will have to find another dog."

After a while they met a small white dog. "I'm sure this dog is very hungry," said Mother. The little dog barked. *Yip-yip-yip.*

"No," said Janet. "That is not a nice dog. I want to give my nice little dog biscuit to a nice little dog."

"Oh, dear," said Mother. "I guess we will have to find another dog."

After a while they met a big black dog. "I'm sure this dog would like two dog biscuits," said Mother.

The dog was hungry. He barked. *Woof-woof-woof.*

"No," said Jimmy. "I don't like dogs that bark."

"Oh, dear," said Mother. "I guess we will have to find another dog."

They went on walking. They met big dogs, little dogs, smooth dogs, curly dogs, dogs that sniffed, and dogs that wagged their tails. Each time they met a dog Jimmy and Janet said, "No, I don't want to give my dog biscuit to this dog."

"Oh, dear," said Mother. "What are we going to do? It's almost time for Daddy to come home, and we have not found the right dog to give the dog biscuits to. What are we going to do?"

Jimmy and Janet thought and thought. What were they going to do? They did not really want to give their dog biscuits to a dog. If Muffy had his own dog biscuits, other dogs must have dog biscuits, too.

"We could give the dog biscuits to a cat," said Janet and laughed. What a funny idea, dog biscuits for a cat!

"Oh, no," said Mother. "A cat couldn't eat a dog biscuit, because it would be too hard for his teeth. Dog biscuits are for dogs." Just the same, on the way home Jimmy and Janet were on the lookout for a cat.

When they were almost home Janet spied a big tiger cat snoozing on a driveway in the sunshine. "There is a cat," she said. "I'm going to give him my dog biscuit."

"I'm afraid that cat does not want your dog biscuit," said Mother.

Janet tiptoed over to the cat and laid her dog biscuit under his nose. "Here is a present for you, kitty," she said.

The cat opened one eye.
He opened the other eye.
He stood up and stretched.
He sniffed the dog biscuit.

Then he sat down and began to eat. It was hard work for him to eat such a hard biscuit, but he crunched and munched and pretty soon the biscuit was gone.

The cat licked his whiskers, looked around, and said, "Meow."

"He liked my dog biscuit," said Janet. "He's saying thank you."

"He wants another dog biscuit," said Jimmy. "Here, kitty. Here is another present for you." The cat crunched and munched Jimmy's dog biscuit, and when it was all gone he sat up and began to wash.

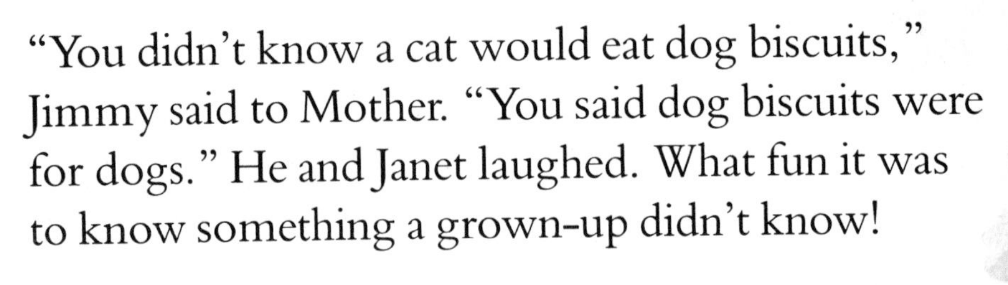

"You didn't know a cat would eat dog biscuits," Jimmy said to Mother. "You said dog biscuits were for dogs." He and Janet laughed. What fun it was to know something a grown-up didn't know!

"No, I didn't know a cat would eat dog biscuits, but now I know it," said Mother, and she laughed, too. "Oh, look, there's Daddy coming home from work."

"Daddy! Daddy!" shouted Janet, running down the sidewalk to meet him. "We gave our dog biscuits to a cat and he ate them!"

"Daddy, Daddy!" shouted Jimmy, running down the sidewalk to meet him. "Mother said the cat wouldn't eat the dog biscuits, but he did! She didn't know!"

Daddy caught Jimmy and Janet and picked them both up at the same time. "Your mother didn't know a cat would eat dog biscuits!" he exclaimed. "What a big joke on Mother!"